EGG

A QUEERED STORY

ROSS VICTORY

Created by J. Ross Victory
rossvictory.com

Cover illustration by David Izaguirre, Jr.
izythereal.com

Cover graphic design and color by William Sikora III
sikoraentertainment.com

Edited and proofread by Kate Seger

Special thanks to all the beta readers
ISBN 13: 978-1-63684-378-0
rossvictory.com

EGG

"Miracle baby" Nakoa Jamar discovers a mosquito bite in the center of his chest on his 12th birthday, which rapidly grows into a Siamese twin. The older Nakoa gets, the more terrorizing his twin brother, Marcus, becomes. Distressed by the changes in their family and unable to bear another scandal incited by Marcus, the Taylors, Nakoa's parents, research doctors to separate the twins after the boys nearly destroy each other in a merciless fight. The problem is the boys are conjoined at the heart. Separation will kill them both.

Using horror, fertility issues, and Yin and Yang symbolism as the backdrop, *Egg* contemplates what it means for light and darkness to manifest in the body. *Egg* explores the limits of love and the limits of hatred while speaking to the ability we have as human beings—the ability to choose.

Content/Trigger Notice

Egg is a horror story that contains graphic descriptions and disturbing content surrounding pregnancy and abuse. The author understands the importance of providing this notice.

*Darkness cannot drive out
darkness; only light can do that.
Hate cannot drive out hate; only
love can do that.*

Martin Luther King, Jr.

WHEN DREAMS BECOME REALITY

"Push!"

A delivery nurse surrounded twenty-five-year-old Shanice Taylor as she screamed, sweat dripping down her forehead, her chin covered in tears and snot.

"Push!"

"I'm pushin'!"

Ron, Shanice's husband, held up her head as she panted. The delivery room had been decorated in canvas paintings of the ocean, with fresh lilies and poinsettias crowding every table and chair in the room, emitting a subtle sweetness into the air. The delivery room was brimming with sunlight and photos of the sea. The air from the air conditioning duct combined with the pictures on the wall and floral aroma created the feel of an island getaway.

"I love you so much, Shanice. So much. You're doing so good," Ron assured his wife, rubbing her back.

A hanging tree branch slammed into the window.

"Ice chips—ice chips!" Shanice mumbled.

Ron fed Shanice ice chips.

"Okay, again, let's push, Mrs. Taylor," the delivery nurse said.

Shanice inhaled deeply. "Ahhhhhhh," she trembled, grasping Ron's hand and the bedpost.

After three miscarriages, and their prior pregnancy ending in a stillbirth on the 30th week, Ron and Shanice remained hopeful for this pregnancy. Having spent twenty thousand dollars on IVF (In Vitro Fertilization) treatments, they vowed this would be their last effort; the struggle to have a child had taken a toll on their marriage.

"Here he comes!" the delivery nurse warned the couple as the baby's head began to crown through Shanice's expanding vagina. The nurse's face suddenly became expressionless. She looked up at the couple creepily for what felt like minutes. Shanice and Ron glanced at each other in panic.

"He's a boy!" the nurse cheered. Ron jumped with excitement.

"A true miracle," Shanice and Ron rejoiced together.

"Do you have a name?"

"Nakoa...'warrior" in Hawaiian. Nakoa Jamar Taylor. Our warrior. Our miracle."

Shanice placed Nakoa on her chest. Nakoa gazed up at his mom with honeysuckled eyes, the size of billiard balls. Nakoa gurgled. Ron fell to his knees, placing his hands up in worship. "Thank you, God," he repeated.

A tree branch slammed into the window, causing everyone to jolt. A nurse adjusted the blinds again before exiting the room leaving the young family to celebrate together.

"I'll text your mom."

Ron picked up his phone to text Shanice's mom about Nakoa's arrival. Scrolling through several unread text messages, Ron clicked open a message from Danica, his ex-girlfriend.

The message read:

Congratulations, Ron, followed by two smile emojis, a smiling witch emoji, and a black heart.

11th BIRTHDAY

The Taylors were a thriving young African-American family living in the upper-middle-class suburb of Peachtree Heights, Atlanta. Landscaped gardens, early-19th century architecture, and great schools were provided exclusively to those who could afford the coveted area.

Shanice and Ron used their connections to purchase their first home in Peachtree. Their house sat at the end of a cul-de-sac complete with a rose garden, an organic vegetable garden, and a picturesque backyard that blended perfectly into a mirror pond before the forest.

Ron and Shanice met each other while obtaining their master's degrees. Ron Taylor was a high-demand employment lawyer. Shanice worked from home selling handmade art online and spent her free time as the face of anti-abortion causes in Georgia, using her story as the primary influencer.

Ron and Shanice spoiled Nakoa, their miracle child, with the best clothes, the highest quality tutors, and the most exclusive kiddie events and toys. Shanice maintained a detailed spreadsheet of every symptom Nakoa had experienced, however subtle, since his birth. As their only son, Ron and Shanice were obsessed with his wellbeing. They arrived early and stayed late at every school event and researched the parents of every childhood friend. The Taylors often vacationed in their Miami beach home to escape the city life of Atlanta. They escaped to their condo in Marseille, France, for more extended vacations, where they also visited Shanice's mother. The Taylors proudly shared professionally photographed holiday cards and digital albums of their family adventures online.

"Hey! No bouncing balls on my new floors."

Nakoa, now ten years old, approaching his 11th birthday, entered the dining room dribbling a basketball followed by his shadow, his dog, Penny. Penny was a lively but sensitive red-coated Welsh Corgi that Nakoa had handpicked from a dog shelter and adopted for his tenth birthday. Nakoa had recently joined "Alley-Oop," a youth basketball league.

"Nakoa Jamar—Ball. Down. Now," Shanice warned, "Are you ready for your game tonight, mister?"

"What's for breakfast, Mom?" Nakoa asked, ignoring his mom's question.

"Your favorite..."

Shanice flipped the last fluffy blueberry pancake onto Nakoa's plate with salmon croquettes.

"My favorite? But, Mom, where are the..."

"...eggs?" Shanice turned off the stove, sprinkling shredded cheddar onto the freshly scrambled eggs as she poured them onto Nakoa's plate.

"You're addicted to these eggs, bud."

Penny cheerfully jumped onto Nakoa's lap. Ron entered the room, kissing his son on the head. He paced over to Shanice, who was pouring the batter into the frying pan. He pressed his waist against Shanice's butt and his lips onto her neck.

"Yours is next, Zaddy." Shanice giggled.

"It better be next."

Nakoa looked on in disgust. For several minutes, the family discussed plans for Nakoa's 11th birthday. Nakoa convinced his parents to allow a supervised movie date between him and his class crush, Perstefania.

12th BIRTHDAY

Penny ran into the kitchen, immediately becoming distracted by her treat dispenser near the refrigerator. Nakoa, on the verge of graduating from middle school, was a straight-A student. He was one of the star players of his youth basketball league. He had recently developed light facial hair under his chin. Although Nakoa was a brewing jock, he was also a nerd. He was addicted to science fiction books and often spent hours online playing remote video games with his friends.

Shanice cracked open two large eggs, which echoed through the kitchen. Ron snuck behind Shanice as she sang Antia Baker's *Rapture of Love.* Ron began to tiptoe his fingers up his wife's sundress as she cooked, popping her underwear strap.

"He's about to be twelve, Ron...now would be a good time to talk to him about ya know...boy body stuff."

"These kids these days know more than I do," Ron responded. "Him and that little girl...what's her name? They're probably already doing it." Shanice looked at her husband, shocked. "If he's my son, he knows what to do."

"Oh my god." She looked over her shoulder for Nakoa before whispering to Ron. "I checked our son's browsing history..."

"Creeper. How about privacy?"

"No! Did you have privacy at eleven?"

She continued, "You should know he searched 'what if I like girls *and* boys.'"

Ron lightly tapped Shanice's butt. He responded, "My boy! Get it where you can get it, son..."

"Ron! If our son is unique, I need to know as soon as possible. I can add it to his chart to document everything. We need to make sure he grows up knowing he can trust us, too."

"The boy can't take a poop without you writing it down! Relax." Ron and Shanice began to bicker about whom would talk to Nakoa about sex.

"You're his father. Please, Ron. His underwear is...changing...too...a lot of boy residue."

Nakoa frolicked in the living room, texting on his new smartphone, scratching his leg.

"Good morning, bud. I have itch cream in my parlor." It was now the peak of summer, and mosquitoes had overtaken Atlanta.

"Who are you texting? Is it..." Shanice paused, scrambling that last bit of egg yolk. "Is Perstefania your girlfriend?"

Ron motioned Shanice to leave him alone.

Nakoa began to forcefully scratch his chest. "Ah, Mom! Cereal!?" Nakoa opened the cereal box and peaked in, still scratching.

"I didn't forget," Shanice began.

Then she screamed, knocking the cereal bowl off the table. A small section in the center of Nakoa's chest began to wrestle around, appearing to move in a circular motion like a finger was trying to poke through Nakoa's polo shirt.

"What?" Nakoa looked up at his mom shyly. Shanice's face became emotionless as she stared at the center of Nakoa's chest.

"What is that—moving—under your shirt?"

Nakoa lowered his chin slowly, keeping his eyes on his mother's face. Frightened as the movement began to sliver like a snake, Nakoa began to flick the outside of his t-shirt. He ran backward, losing his balance. He knocked over dishes and a large bowl of Granny Smith apples.

The movement under his shirt stopped. Ron began to comfort his wife and son. "If it's a spider, we'll kill it, okay."

"Lift up your shirt, bud..."

Nakoa raised his shirt over his face. Ron, Shanice, and Nakoa stood frozen for several minutes as Ron's face went through several emotions. Ron glanced at his wife, who stood behind Nakoa. Penny pranced behind Shanice, wagging her tail excitedly. Shanice furrowed her eyebrows.

A human face—the size of a walnut—with menacing eyes appeared on the head of a bright red bite in the center of Nakoa's chest. Its bloodshot eyes staring back at Ron. The face zig-zagged its mouth from side to side, making slurping sounds and coughing. Teeth formed quickly as the head moved in maniacal circles.

"Ron?"

The more the head twisted, the more human-like the bite became. Its head soon had a neck. Through puss and blood, shoulders sprouted as its upper limbs appeared to climb through Nakoa's chest cavity.

Ron lowered Nakoa's shirt. He reached for his phone near the sink.

"Who are you calling?" Shanice demanded as Ron flubbed his cell phone.

Nakoa stood calmly in the center of the kitchen, beginning to scratch his chest again. His mother lifted up his shirt, then instantly lowered it, covering her mouth.

"Don't scratch, sit down," Nakoa's dad warned.

Shanice began to laugh. Penny started to growl and bark. Shanice's laugh became uncontrollable before she stopped, regaining composure. She grabbed a carving knife from her knife block. The sharpness of the blade against the wooden block frightened Nakoa.

"What are you gonna do?" Ron asked.

"I'm gonna cut it off my son."

"No," Ron cautioned. "We need to go to the ER or something."

Shanice paced the kitchen with the knife raised. Penny growled uncontrollably as the family argued. Nakoa stood, helplessly terrified. His shirt began to rise upward toward the ceiling by itself.

"Call the ER and say what? A face is growing on our son's chest?"

"Uhh...yeah," Ron said.

"No, no—let me think..."

"Dadddddd," Nakoa wailed. "Owwww!!"

The protruding head became arm's length. Skin cells and fat dripped on the floor. Facial features were discernible through Nakoa's t-shirt as a torso rose from his chest. His t-shirt stuck on the torso's back.

The doorbell rang. Shanice belted out laughter before covering her face and beginning to panic. Penny ran to the front door, barking.

The doorbell rang again.

"We're going to the ER!" Ron took off to his bedroom to get his car keys. Shanice tried to calm her son while suppressing her vomit.

14th BIRTHDAY

The unfathomable became a reality. Within a couple of years—long, exhausting years—the inexplicable had normalized. News reporters and journalists worldwide crowded the Taylor's lawn every day to get a photograph of Nakoa and his brother emerging from his chest. The family decided to call it Marcus.

Marcus's torso extended nearly three feet from Nakoa's chest, leaning to the right, and had grown to match Nakoa's height at five foot eight inches. While both boys were slim in build, they weighed almost two hundred and fifty pounds together. Because of their weight and lopsided shape, they could not stand for longer than twenty minutes. Shanice handmade their clothes.

After years of doctor visits and global interest, Nakoa and Marcus were considered an unprecedented case; they were the first of their kind. Anatomists developed the term: **Postnatal, pre-adolescent, thoracic rapid Siamese twin birth** to describe the boys. Ron and Shanice had released their IVF provider of liability nearly fourteen years ago and scrambled to find support from the medical community.

Each day required a strategic level of planning for the family to avoid the media. It had been nearly two years since the family had done an interview. It had been over a year since a photo had been published of Nakoa and Marcus. Cable news reported suspicion from the general public that the boys did not exist. A popular conspiracy theory about "a pharmaceutical experiment gone wrong" had developed and gained momentum in online forums and social media. Politicians began to campaign for government regulation of vaccines and pharmaceuticals using Nakoa's and Marcus's unusual case.

Nakoa had experienced five panic attacks and suffered from low-grade depression after Marcus's arrival. For nearly six months, every night, Nakoa would wake up screaming in delirium to see another human, Marcus, emerging from his chest. Shanice hired psychologists and psychiatrists from every specialization to help Nakoa cope with what he experienced.

None of them could help him. His problem was just too unusual, and Marcus disrupted every therapy session he was put in. Nakoa grew more and more withdrawn and traumatized as his twin grew stronger. It was as if his twin was leeching energy from him.

"I'm sorry," the last psychologist she called said as he packed up to leave. "I don't think there's anything I can do here. Your son is in for a rough time. But he's not troubled or crazy. He's reacting to a legitimately terrible situation. The one thing I can think of to do is remove the twin. That's the only thing that will make him feel better."

Shanice had started setting money aside for pricey experimental surgery, but even with Ron's income, they weren't there yet. She sat down across from her son at the dinner table that night and tried to talk with him about what he was experiencing.

"I know this is hard, honey," she said, but Marcus cut her off.

"Hard!" he squawked. "This is great! Three meals a day, everyone's trying to talk to me about my feelings...I feel like a million bucks!"

Shanice pursed her lips. "I'm not talking to you. I'm trying to speak with my son—"

"Don't you get it, lady? I AM your son. We're one and the same. Can't get one without the other."

"We did get one without the other for twelve years," Shanice said. "And we hope we can go back to that very, very soon."

"Leave it, Mom," Nakoa said as Marcus cackled maniacally. "It's not going to do any good. He can't be reasoned with."

"We're going to get rid of this creature," Shanice said. "One way or another. Don't worry, baby. We're here for you."

Marcus just rolled his eyes and took a big bite of spaghetti. He and Nakoa shared a stomach, so he didn't really need to eat. But he liked the taste of food and being sloppy just to be annoying.

The Taylors had gone through fifteen different homeschool teachers. Every teacher quit after being bullied or terrorized by Marcus. Marcus was loud and rude. Most teachers, and psychologists, were simply too frightened by the twins' appearance to continue their work. Only one teacher survived the twins. A muscular man teacher called Abraham, also a twin brother, had worked for the Taylors for seven months before quitting to take care of his aging mother.

Marcus had driven one teacher to tears after commenting that she was shaped like a giraffe because of her long neck, full of varicose veins, and a lower belly pooch that sat above her thin legs. After Nakoa reasoned with Marcus to calm down, Nakoa asked for a break to speak to Marcus privately. The teacher refused the break. Marcus stood up in a fit of anger, overpowering the body's nervous system and releasing the boys' full bowels on the kitchen floor as Penny looked on.

Ron and Shanice's decision to homeschool the boys came from a flood of rage instigated by a low quiz score. Marcus stabbed the teacher repeatedly with sharp pencils causing lead poisoning and an expensive lawsuit resulting in the forced sale of the family's French vacation property.

Shanice wept when she learned that they would have to sell. She'd loved that property—and more than that, she'd loved the idea of being the sort of person who owned a house in France. Yet another thing Marcus had taken from them.

Not only was he mean-spirited, but he was moody. If Nakoa said *"up,"* Marcus said, *"down."* If Nakoa liked you, Marcus burned with hatred. When Nakoa had a lousy day, Marcus was agreeable and easy to talk to. Despite this, both boys were pleasant during breakfast and had become addicted to eggs.

15th BIRTHDAY

As the boys became older, Nakoa slowly became introverted and more visibly embarrassed about Marcus. Nakoa's eyes often looked empty and soulless. Most nights he cried himself to sleep or struggled to fall asleep. He was overcome with feelings of shame and worthlessness. He made slow progress with understanding what had happened to him and lacked interest in life most days because of the isolation.

Nakoa tried to seek peace with Marcus instead of arguing or trying to change him, which exhausted him. The boys had formed a loose agreement that only one of them would speak in front of their parents, tutors, and visitors. By not speaking at the same time, they discovered people felt more comfortable in their presence, which Marcus hated. Nakoa proposed that they form a daily schedule in which one boy would cover their face and body while the other boy was being social, which Marcus refused. Privately, Marcus claimed that Nakoa was scared of his emotions and responded from his head instead of their heart.

"Why do you care so much what people think about us?" Marcus would ask.

"Stop saying 'us' you mean YOU."

Nakoa rejected that they were related, let alone the same person, often referring to Marcus as a creature and IT. Marcus blamed Nakoa's discomfort with their situation on Nakoa's self-hatred and poor communication skills. Marcus frequently referenced himself as part of Nakoa and vice versa, citing that he could sense when their environment triggered an emotion.

Marcus's antics became more manipulative and pre-meditative by the day as Nakoa tried laboriously to feel better. Marcus graduated from an out-of-control teenager to an evil one. Marcus discovered that he could fully operate Nakoa's lower limbs if Nakoa was asleep. Marcus would crush sleeping pills and mix them into Nakoa's dinner when he looked away. Thinking he had overeaten, Nakoa would request to lay down, and Marcus would take over the legs.

On the night before Nakoa's 15th birthday, Marcus drugged his brother with sleeping pills. After Ron and Shanice fell asleep, Marcus began to explore the home, searching for Penny.

"Hey, girl?" Marcus peeked behind corners and paced the home as his giant double-torso shadow moved from room to room against nightlights. Asleep, Nakoa's limp neck bobbed from side to side.

"Penny? Here, girl…" Penny's collar jingled softly. Her paws scratched the floors lightly as she trodded through the home to escape Marcus's voice before being trapped in the living room.

Penny, tail down, shyly backed away from Marcus. She faced the wall watching Marcus approach her through the corners of her unblinking eyes.

"Do you hear me calling you?" Marcus grabbed Penny and flung her across the room. She belted as her small body hit the corner of the fireplace.

"You fucking bitch." Marcus laughed. The last embers of the fireplace crackled in the background. The shadow of the double torso grew against the brick façade as Marcus neared Penny. She lay on her back, shivering in shock.

"Annoying dog. He loves you 'so so much.'" Marcus rolled his eyes. He paced around Penny, who looked away, avoiding eye contact with him. Penny glanced at Nakoa as he slept and barked.

"Look at ME bitch!" Marcus grabbed Penny's snout, knocking Nakoa's head against the wall. Nakoa yawned and smacked his lips before returning to sleep.

"Look at ME!" Penny panted through Marcus's fist, which held her snout close.

Marcus roared as he stomped on Penny's chest, snapping her ribs, which popped individually like tiny compacted firecrackers.

"MEEEE!"

Penny's body began to convulse as she tried to inhale through her smashed lungs, several ribs poking through her flesh and fur. Marcus stomped on Penny again, snapping her neck. He used the weight of his legs to separate her small head from her body.

Marcus stomped on what was left of Penny. Every stomp harder and more resolute than the last, jumping on her skull for several minutes until all that remained of Penny was compacted bloody flesh and hair. He dragged his fingers across the piano keys. The living room light turned on.

Marcus turned around as Nakoa woke up. Ron, the boy's father, stared at the boys from across the living room in shock.

"What the..." Ron demanded.

Marcus wiped his mouth with his fist, smiling embarrassedly. Nakoa looked over at the splotch of blood on the carpet. He stared at the flesh and fur swinging from his shoe. Nakoa instinctively understood what happened, becoming overwhelmed with sadness, falling to the ground sobbing.

How could he have done this? If Marcus was part of him, that meant that he was partly responsible for what had happened. Had he secretly wanted to do this to Penny all along?

"Sorry, guys," Marcus smirked. "Got a little out of control there. Won't happen again."

Ron stared at his son's twin, appalled and horrified. Then, he made a decision.

"We're going to clean this up," he said, hustling toward the hall closet for a mop and bucket. "And we're not going to tell your mom what happened. Understand?"

"Thanks, Pops," Marcus rasped. "Appreciate it."

"We're really going to lie to Mom?" Nakoa said, wiping the tears from his face. "Won't she be really mad when she finds out?"

"Son, if there's one thing I've learned, it's that sometimes you can't tell the whole truth. Sometimes little secrets can be better than the truth if it protects someone's feelings. Not big ones—never big ones. But your mother would be heartbroken if she found out what happened here. You wouldn't want to hurt your mom, would you?"

"No," Nakoa said hesitantly. "Of course not."

"Well then, there we go," Ron said. "We'll think of a story to tell her. I'll work on it while I'm mopping."

"Okay," Nakoa said, trying not to look at Marcus's grinning face next to him.

It didn't feel right to lie to his mother. Not at all. But if his dad was pushing for it, maybe it was the right thing to do. But Shanice loved Penny. Penny might as well have been her daughter.

16th BIRTHDAY

Nakoa and Marcus entered the kitchen for breakfast. The atmosphere in the home had become ominous. Responses were altered to avoid provoking Marcus, resulting in periods of prolonged silence. Every new item Ron or Shanice had purchased for themselves—from shoes to electronics—were hidden and locked in their basement. Nakoa communicated with his parents through text messages. Ron and Shanice tended to avoid the boys if it wasn't necessary to be in their presence.

"Let's do something fun for your birthday—it's been a while since we've done something as a family." Ron offered suggestions on birthday activities for several minutes. Everyone sat in silence.

"Maybe another pet?" Shanice asked. "Ever since Penny ran away, it's been quiet around here."

Nakoa and Marcus's heads both looked away as Ron watched them.

"I miss grandma," Nakoa blurted.

"And she misses you." Shanice reached for Nakoa's hand.

"Can I be excused?"

The boys got up and walked away to the bathroom. Nakoa began running the bathwater. He removed his clothes, looking at his reflection with shame and disgust.

"Have I ever told you we have a small dick?" Marcus told his brother. "You'd think it'd grow by now," Marcus added as he observed their penis.

Drenched in silence, the twins entered the foaming bathwater looking at each other with palpable hatred.

"You never shut up. Can you be silent for a day? An hour? A minute?" The boys began to switch temperaments, Nakoa's voice rising.

"You've ruined my life! My family hates me because of you! I have no friends because of you! I can't play basketball! Perstefania dumped me because now I'm a freak! We are famous because of you! You murdered my dog! All my problems are because of YOU!" Nakoa's anger began to grow and radiate from his eyes.

"But I *am* you," Marcus said calmly. "We have the same heart. I'm the Yin; you're the Yang. Most people never acknowledge their shadow. Here I am." Marcus giggled.

Nakoa began to tremble on the verge of rage. "Oh my god, shut up!!!"

"Perstefania is a nice girl. And I've noticed we're bisexual—don't worry, I won't tell Mom and Dad."

"No, I'm not! Why do you keep saying we, we, we? You mean YOU!" Nakoa's temper continued to expand as Marcus's tone softened.

"Abraham? The muscular teacher? Green eyes? Canons in his arms…"

"I'm not. Shut up, freak!" Nakoa shouted.

Marcus continued, "Our heart is the same. When you lie, I speak the truth. When you love, I am angry. You can hate me, but you just hate yourself."

Nakoa covered his ears in aggravation. "I'd cut you off and burn you if I could. You are nothing to me."

"You feel like we are ugly to look at, but everyone has light and darkness inside them. Is it better to see me or to be blind?"

Pretending to reach for a towel, Nakoa hastily changed direction and leaned over on his stomach, placing Marcus's face and torso under the bathwater. Nakoa used his body weight to begin to drown Marcus, placing his hands around his throat. As Marcus lost consciousness, Nakoa would too and fall into the water.

For several minutes, the twins flipped each other over and over, losing consciousness, fighting each other's nervous system for control of their body.

The bathroom door cracked open.

"Honey, what's all the noi…" Shanice opened the door all the way to see Marcus positioned on top of Nakoa.

"Ron!" Shanice belted. Shanice punched Marcus in the face, breaking his nose and lifting Nakoa from underneath the bathwater, which became red-colored.

"Nakoa tried to drown ME!"

Shanice socked Marcus in the face again. "I've had it with you! Ron! It's drowning our son... Ron!" she screamed, burning in anger.

"No, no! He tried to drown me..."

"I've almost found out how to get rid of you," Shanice warned Marcus. "Don't you ever touch my son again!"

"Nah!" Marcus said. "Get out of here, you old bitch! You can't tell me what to do!"

Shanice backed away from the boys, frightened, as Ron ran into the room.

"He's horrible!" she sobbed. "This thing is horrible! I can't live like this, Ron! We have to find a solution!" Shanice's sob shifted into a painful wail as she fell to the floor.

Her husband dragged the boys out of the bathtub and handed Nakoa a towel. Marcus leered at Shanice, eyebrows waggling creepily, and she stormed out of the room, leaving Ron alone with the twins.

"Your mother—" he started to say, but Marcus cut in.

"Bet she leaves," he brayed. "Bet she doesn't stick around. Mark my words. She'll leave you, Ron. She'll leave all of us. She's the type. When the going gets tough, like the Road Runner!" Marcus made a loud bing sound.

Ron looked at Marcus, disturbed.

"Don't listen to him, Dad!" Nakoa said. "He's just trying to mess with your head. He'll tell you anything that he thinks will freak you out and piss you off. Just don't speak."

"Right," Ron said, but his eyes were dead and empty, and all the fight had gone out of him. It was as if Marcus had confirmed something he'd long suspected—like he touched a hidden wound.

"Dad?"

"Go to your room, son. We can work this out tomorrow. I promise."

Nakoa wobbled to his room, feeling uneasy. His twin's evil laughter rang in his ears. Nakoa seethed in anger as he heard Ron comforting Shanice in the background, his mom begging for Marcus's removal.

17ᵗʰ BIRTHDAY

"Good morning." Shanice calmly set the table for breakfast. She did not make eye contact with Nakoa or Marcus, who now had a visible scar on his nose from his mother. Shanice's phone illuminated with a text as she began to place oranges in the juicer. While Nakoa was busy texting Perstefania, Marcus swiped open the phone to read an email from Dr. Henry Thompson.

I took a look at the past and current X-rays for Nakoa's and Marcus's body. Both boys share an adult-sized heart and vital organs. One heart supplies blood to 1.5 human bodies. Nakoa's heart has become abnormally enlarged. The twin who does not possess immediate access to the digestive organs and lower limbs has an absolute fatality rate by separating them. Still, with separation, Nakoa would inherit an imminent risk of congestive heart failure.

Marcus put the phone back to sleep before Shanice turned around.

"Ten scrambled eggs, just the way my boys like them." Shanice smiled and giggled, making extended eye contact with Marcus.

Shanice took her phone to check the notification. Ron entered the kitchen without making eye contact with the boys. Shanice called Ron over to view the message on her cell phone as Marcus watched them bicker. Shanice and Ron had been aggressively contacting doctors around the world after the bathtub incident. Shanice spent hours and hours on the phone and online to find a solution—any solution they could afford. The answer was always the same: *They're joined at the heart. This has never been done before. Both will die.*

Her stomach dropped, and her eyes filled with tears. She'd suffered for years with this awful creature in her house, but she'd always held out hope that there was some way to get rid of him. That somehow, some experimental treatment, even a shady doctor in an alley somewhere, would be the answer. This was a crushing blow.

Dr. Henry Thompson had been her final chance. He was the last doctor who'd been willing to take on this case. If he wasn't able to help, no one would.

"Everything okay...Mom?" Marcus said, his voice cruel and mocking. She knew he must have read the message on her phone.

"Yes," she said without turning around. "Everything's fine."

"Well, it's not fine with me," Marcus responded." I just found out my mom's trying to kill me. Did you know about that...Mom?"

Shanice clenched her jaw, not trusting herself to respond.

"My own mother!" Marcus said. "What do you think of that? Wonder what would happen if I called a reporter and brought in the media?" Marcus motioned his hands into the air. "Neurotic mother plots to murder twin son in sleep."

"Shut up!" Shanice and Nakoa screamed at the same time.

Marcus looked at his twin, stunned. "You're on her side, traitor?"

Shanice stormed out of the room, not wanting Marcus to see her cry. He'd just make fun of her if he did.

She couldn't live like this. She couldn't live without hope that she'd be able to get rid of Marcus to get her son back. But she didn't know what else she could do. She couldn't abandon Nakoa. He was her only son, her miracle baby, and he needed her now more than ever.

Collapsing on her bed, she burst into hopeless tears.

ONE MONTH BEFORE 18th BIRTHDAY

"Hun, I gotta tell you something," Ron said as Shanice adjusted her dress in their oversized Venetian marble mirror.

"I know...eighteen years...I can barely believe it either," Shanice responded.

"When we were younger, trying to start a family for years, doing what we thought was best..."

Shanice tilted her head in suspicion.

"I only wanted what was best..." Ron paused, then said, "We wanted a child so bad! It worked for twelve years."

Shanice looked at her husband, confused. "It worked?"

"Okay..." Ron took a deep breath. "Do you remember Danica?"

"Your ex?" Shanice became agitated. Ron sat down, placing his head in his arms.

"Did you cheat on me with Danica, Ron!? After all of this, you cheat on me? Fucking loser." Shanice shoved her husband in his stomach.

"Noooooo, but I didn't tell you everything about her." Ron gazed out the bedroom window. "She has...abilities. She helps people...with...*alternative* methods." Ron paused. "I thought she could help us."

"Alternative methods? What did you do!?" Shanice screamed. "Oh my god. What. Did. You. Do?" She closed her eyes, anticipating Ron's response while beginning to tap her foot. She looked over at him, shaking her head in disbelief. "Abilities? Alternative methods? What did you do?"

"I asked Danica to do a fertility spell...so we could have a family."

"A what?" Shanice asked. "Why would we need a *witch* for help when we paid twenty thousand dollars for IVF?"

"We wanted a child so bad. After all the miscarriages, after the stillbirth..." Ron began. "I wanted to make you happy, to guarantee the family we dreamt about."

Shanice grabbed a photo of Nakoa and Marcus, shoving it in Ron's face. "Is this what you meant!?" Ron looked away as Shanice put the picture against his face.

"What did she do? Did you give her a piece of my hair? A nail? Did you feed me something? Did you drug me, Ron?" Shanice asked.

"An egg."

Shanice laughed. "Haha, an egg." She gazed at him in disbelief. "Ya know, you were always acting so nonchalant. From the moment you saw IT in your son's chest, you were so calm...almost like you expected it."

"Danica warned that we could not have light without the dark," Ron continued.

"You didn't ask her what the fuck she meant? If I were part of the decision to poison me, I would have asked that." Shanice paced around the bedroom in anger. "Did you expect her to just tell you a monster will grow out of your son's chest when he enters puberty?"

"I thought it was gonna be some type of mood thing or personality thing. Not...a person..."

"You 'thought,'" Shanice said in air quotes.

For several minutes Ron expressed his intentions to his wife. Shanice and Ron had been arguing so long that they were late for breakfast. Nakoa and Marcus approached their parents' locked bedroom door. They tried to listen to the conversation through the wall.

Shanice chuckled to herself. "Am I even alive right now?" Shanice got in Ron's face counting the incidents. "Penny...oh, I know, Nakoa texted me. That's unrecoverable, Ron. Shits on the floor in front of the teacher. Stabs the teacher. Reminder—lawsuit cost us hundreds of thousands of dollars, and she could have *died*."

Shanice continued, "IT nearly drowned your son. We have been alienated from our jobs, family, and friends—where is the light, Ron? All I see is darkness. You should have let me cut it off."

"I just wanted us to have a family," Ron repeated over and over.

"And you didn't bother with the details. This isn't a tarot card, Ron...this is real witchcraft. This is your son's life. Our legacy." Shanice startled herself. "Wa—wait! Why are you telling me now? So suing the IVF provider was a whole song and dance?"

"Yes," Ron said. "It was Danica. I'm so sorry. After everything happened, I didn't want to admit the truth. And one lie just led to another. At some point, I just committed to the fake story I'd created."

"You're nuts, Ron! Both of us are literally headcases."

"I know. Shanice, I know."

Marcus and Nakoa were still listening to their parents' conversation through the wall. Marcus snickered cruelly at the desperate tone in Ron's voice.

"Dad's in trouble now!" he said. "He's really stepped in it."

"Shut up!" Nakoa said.

"How do you feel about the fact that this is all Dad's fault? Feel good?"

"Shut up, shut up, shut up!"

"You've got to make this right, Ron," Shanice said. "Find Danica and get her to undo the spell."

"I can't," Ron replied. "I haven't spoken to her for like eighteen years. Not since our son was born. Now I can't find her at all. I've searched for her online every day since Marcus appeared, but there's no trace of her anywhere."

"Sounds about right. Witches are probably good at disappearing!" Shanice interjected.

"I've called her old number, sent her emails, even stopped by her old place. She hasn't responded to anything. There are new people living in her apartment. Her phone number is disconnected. She seems to have totally gone off the grid."

"If you don't find her, I will. And I will warn you once, if you think what happened to Penny was disappointing, wait until I find that heffer. Find her!" Shanice said. "Whatever it takes, Ron." She continued, "You did whatever it takes to get pregnant, so now you need to do whatever it takes to fix this."

And with that, she turned on her heel and walked upstairs without giving her husband another look. She passed by her twin sons, and Marcus flashed her a sinister smile. He wagged his tongue.

"Leave my mom alone!" Nakoa said.

"I'll do what I want," Marcus said.

Ron knew his wife was right. It was his responsibility to fix the situation. While he'd already been looking for Danica, now he kicked his search into high gear.

He spent hundreds of hours on the internet, speaking to people who performed fertility spells and egg rituals and hundreds of hours reading online forums.

He asked detailed and probing questions, trying to see if anyone had dealt with anything like this before. At first, it seemed like his search was going nowhere. No one had ever heard of an evil twin popping out of a child's chest. In fact, most of the people in the forums didn't seem like real witches at all. They were just internet fakes with Halloween-themed profile images.

Then, one day, Ron noticed a new response from a username he'd never seen before.

"It's rare," the message said, "but it can happen. In fact, I've seen it myself. Just once."

The poster ended their message with two smiling emojis, a witch emoji, and a black heart. Just like Danica had.

Their username was "Ambrosia"—but he knew that Danica might be writing under a false name. This was the internet.

Heart pounding, he typed a response.

"I had an ex-girlfriend once who used the same string of emojis in her messages," he said. "She did me a big favor once. But it came with strings attached."

The response came almost immediately.

"Hi, Ron."

"Danica!? I need to speak with you. Can we meet?"

He assumed she already knew why he needed to talk. His posts were all over the forum.

"Fine," she said. "I'll talk. I know you've been looking for me."

Ron logged off and almost sprinted to break the news to his wife. He thought she'd be happy, but she looked disgusted when she heard what Danica had said.

"Go get my son back. And if she says you gotta fuck her, you better fuck her like his life depends on it. Fix this now, or I'll remove IT myself, and it won't be pretty." Shanice glared at Ron, sending chills down his arms. "And I may just remove you, too."

TWO NIGHTS BEFORE 18th BIRTHDAY

Ron drove overnight to the neighboring state of South Carolina to meet with his ex-girlfriend, Danica, now Ambrosia, to explain what had occurred. She'd privately messaged him her address right after their conversation. He frowned when he saw that she'd moved out of state. How had he not known that?

He drove ten miles over the speed limit the whole time and made the entire trip in under three hours. Finally, he pulled up outside a ramshackle three-story house in the middle of a dense forest. It looked exactly like the sort of place a witch would live. *Damn, so I dated an actual witch.* Ron thought as he approached the property.

When Ambrosia saw him, she sprinted down the steps. He hadn't seen her in almost twenty years, but she looked exactly the same as she had when they first parted ways. In fact, she looked better. Ron wondered if she was using some kind of anti-aging potion or if unnatural youth was just a normal witch thing.

"Ron!" she said, wrapping her arms around him and holding him close.

But he was in no mood to get a hug from his ex-girlfriend. He roughly shoved her away, overwhelmed and panicked by the state of his family.

"How could you do this, Danica?" he said. "This is my only son. Now he has this—thing—growing out of his chest. It's ruined our lives. It's ruining my marriage. It's ruining my work. It has to go. You have to help us."

"I'm sorry, Ron. I did try to warn you—"

"You didn't try hard enough! This is all your fault!"

"Magic isn't free, Ron. There's always a cost," Ambrosia said as her excitement to see Ron deflated.

"Well, this is too expensive!"

Ambrosia sighed. "Let's go get something to eat. There's a spot around here that makes breakfast croissants just the way you like them. There's no point in discussing this on an empty stomach."

They went to a diner, but things were no better there. The ex-couple soon began to argue about instances in their past relationship when Ron had been selfish, which paralleled the state of Ron and Shanice's marriage.

"You never came to any of my art shows!" Ambrosia said, feeling like a fool as she allowed herself to get sucked in, yet again, to an argument with her ex-boyfriend.

"I was busy! I'm a high-powered lawyer. I was working to support us—both of us. I didn't have time to go to some tiny gallery to see pictures on a wall."

"Pictures on a wall? It was important to me!" Ambrosia said. "I went to every event you asked me to go to. That wasn't exactly fun for me...all the fake laughing and god-awful high heels, but that's what good partners do...and then you dumped me out of nowhere!"

"It wasn't out of nowhere, Ambrosia. I just didn't see a future together."

"It hurt. It really hurt. And you know, the breakup is why I started practicing magic in the first place."

"What?" Ron said, setting his fork down on his plate.

"I did it to cope with the pain that you left me with," Ambrosia said, feeling frustrated. She was pouring her heart out to her ex, and he was stonewalling her.

"Well, that was very irresponsible, Danica," Ron said smugly. "Normal people see a therapist or call a friend or a family member. I don't know why you thought becoming a...witch...would be a smart thing to do after breaking up."

Ambrosia had prepared herself to confess to Ron that he was the love of her life, and she had never been able to move on from him. Ambrosia had compared every person to Ron, and they never measured up. It was becoming increasingly clear that a confession wasn't going to happen. Ambrosia continued to wait for opportunities to tell Ron.

"Magic is dangerous," he said. "Have you tried therapy? Therapy is a reasonable thing to do when bad things happen. For example, my son is in therapy...because there is a HUMAN growing out of him. Witchcraft? Nah."

"You're the one who asked me to put a spell on Shanice! I was just living my life."

"And you should never have agreed to do that," Ron said, crossing his arms. "With great power comes great responsibility. And then you didn't even explain, coherently, what you were doing."

Becoming annoyed by Ron's lecture and insensitivity, Ambrosia handed him a large black box with an egg surrounded by thick padding. She angrily wrote the instructions on a napkin as Ron spoke.

"I don't have to deal with you. I've suffered enough." She wrote frantically on several napkins before continuing, "Feed this egg to both boys on Nakoa's 18th birthday. The napkins have the conditions."

Ambrosia slammed the napkin down before packing up her items. She continued, "Give them water from the mirror pond in your backyard when they eat it. Marcus will go away."

"How will he go away?"

"Does it matter?" Ambrosia responded before standing up and storming out of the restaurant. Once outside, she held back tears while waiting for her taxi.

Ron, who became frustrated, grabbed the napkins off the table and stuffed them into his pocket. He peeked at the egg before paying his tab and driving back to Atlanta.

Within hours, he entered his large home carrying the oversized box as Shanice waited watching TV.

"This is it." Ron revealed the egg to Shanice. They whispered in the kitchen.

"Anything else, Ron? Tell me exactly what she said."

Ron contemplated telling Shanice about the argument. "She said that if we have children again, it will happen again. We need to use this egg and water from the pond in the back, and Marcus will go away."

"Did she ask you to..." Shanice glanced at Ron's lap. "I don't care. I just want to know."

"No!"

On Nakoa's 18th birthday, the family woke up like they usually did. Shanice prepared breakfast, mixing in the magical egg into the twins' food.

"What should we do for your birthday?" Both parents stared at the twins as Ron filled their plates with magical eggs. Shanice irritatedly grabbed the plates from Ron, slamming them on the table and smiling. Nakoa sat, texting Perstefania, and Marcus sat bored and agitated for no reason.

"I wanna lay down," Nakoa said after they'd finished breakfast.

"Of course, honey, go lay down." Shanice removed the empty plates, placing them in the sink. Ron and Shanice, overcome with pity and concern, watched the twins as they left the kitchen to take a nap.

Suddenly, they were jolted awake. Marcus began to panic as the muscles and tissue surrounding the insertion point began to contract. His torso began to tremble as he stared at Nakoa.

"I am the Yin; you are the Yang," Marcus said as he became smaller. "You are the light; I am the darkness. I will live inside of you."

Within two hours, Marcus had nearly fully retracted into Nakoa's chest. Nakoa watched in disbelief. Marcus told Nakoa repeatedly that he would always exist and could never be ignored. Soon, all that remained was Marcus's tiny hand protruding from Nakoa's chest, reaching out for one last moment. The hand retracted slowly until Marcus's index finger, the size of a speck, curled into Nakoa's torso, closing up to become a bright red bite.

Nakoa rubbed the bite mark with mingled emotions of sadness, anxiety, and relief before being prompted to use the restroom.

Ron knocked on his son's bedroom door. Shanice busted through the door, embracing her son tightly for several minutes, touching his chest, and kissing his forehead.

"I've missed you so much," Shanice said. "So much!"

Ron rubbed his son's head and back. He could hardly believe it. At last—at long last—the family's six-year nightmare was over. He'd solved the problem, with a little help from Ambrosia. He felt like a hero as he stroked Nakoa's hair. Things could go back to normal now. His marriage was saved, and they could forget this nightmare.

Shanice was much more ambivalent. Ron had broken her trust—and even though he'd had plenty of opportunities over the years to come clean and admit the truth, he chose to double down on the lies. She felt like she'd spent the last twenty years married to a stranger. Had she ever really known her husband at all? She was beyond elated that Nakoa was saved, yet she didn't know how to move forward. She felt lost. How could they ever go back to normal after everything that had happened? How could she ever respect Ron and trust him to protect her and her son?

Nakoa didn't know how he felt. His twin had made his life a living hell for years. But he couldn't see this as a happy ending. Part of him kept thinking about everything that he'd lost since his twelfth birthday. He'd been so innocent then, so certain that things would turn out well for him and that he'd take the world by storm. Now he wasn't so sure. Thanks to Marcus, he had no friends, no romantic relationship, and his confidence had taken a hit. He was plagued by the question, *"What am I?"* as his identity was one of coping with Marcus.

He hadn't been to school in years. And he wasn't fully sure that his twin wouldn't come back someday—disturbed by predictions and statements Marcus had made for years. After all, Marcus appeared out of nowhere. Who was to say he wasn't just dormant, biding his time and waiting for the moment he could screw up Nakoa's life again?

Nakoa didn't tell his parents any of what he was feeling, though. He didn't want to worry them. Marcus haunted his dreams for months after he disappeared. Nakoa would sit bolt upright in bed, choking back a scream, certain he'd see his twin's eyes staring back at him out of the darkness.

He would have nightmares of Marcus emerging from the chest of strangers. From the cashier at a coffee shop to an elderly woman waiting at a bus stop, Marcus popped into Nakoa's dreams when he least expected him. He once dreamt that his dog Penny had returned to him, only to discover Marcus emerging from Penny's chest. Marcus's final words stayed with him always: *"I will live inside of you."*

19th BIRTHDAY

After years of dealing with Marcus's cruelty, Nakoa was slowly recovering. He was just about to start attending high school again. Ron and Shanice had decided to transfer him to a new school, much to Nakoa's dismay. He'd hoped to reunite with Perstefania and all his old friends again.

"Honey, I think it's time for a fresh start," his mother said, setting a plate of eggs down on the table. "You've been through so much. Do you really want to constantly be reminded of...you know who...every time you go to class? Do you want people to constantly be asking about him in the hallways?"

"I don't care," Nakoa said. "He's gone now. I just want my life back or a new life."

"You will get it back. Once you're in a new place. Now, eat your breakfast."

Nakoa scowled down at his plate, but he ate his eggs with gusto. Shanice looked anxiously at her husband as he sat down across from her.

They'd been having issues ever since she'd learned about the fertility spell. She couldn't comprehend he'd done that without consulting her. It felt invasive and belligerent—after all, she'd been the one who'd had to carry the baby. Had she been under Danica's creepy magical influence throughout her entire pregnancy?

Ron met her gaze, and eventually, she got up to drive Nakoa to school. She knew that what had happened wasn't her fault—but she felt guilty about it as if she'd failed to protect her son from harm somehow. She'd thought she'd anticipated everything, but who could have expected an evil Siamese twin to pop out of her son's chest and make everyone's life a living hell? Now she was determined to give Nakoa whatever he needed to get his life back on track.

"Thanks for the ride, Mom," Nakoa said as he got out of the car, eyes downcast. He didn't want to start over. He wanted things to be the same as they were before. Although he was now nineteen, he wanted to experience being a teenager.

At least, if things went well, he'd only have to spend one year in his new school. No one would know his true age, and no one would think of him as a freak. Then he could move on to college and reinvent himself. He was looking forward to it and was determined to study hard. Whatever it took.

To his surprise, Nakoa enjoyed his classes. Everyone at school was warm and friendly. It wasn't like before when everyone had been scared of him and disgusted by the evil twin sticking out of his chest and the associated smell.

By the end of the day, he felt much better. His backpack was heavy with all the extra books he was bringing home. He was behind the other students—in some classes, very behind—but his teachers saw his potential, and they were all encouraging. He knew that if he worked at it, he could get back on track.

Ron and Shanice's day didn't go as well as their son's. As soon as Shanice got back to the house, she turned to face her husband, hands on her hips.

"Ron, this isn't working," she said.

He looked back at her blankly, looking stricken.

"I can't get over what you did," she went on. "Getting your ex-girlfriend to put a spell on me? Without telling me? You clearly didn't think about the consequences at all."

"Shanice, I'm—I'm sorry—"

"I know you are. And I know you had no way of knowing what would happen. Or how horrible the fallout would be for us. That's why I've tried to get over it. I've tried as hard as I could. But I can't, Ron. I just can't. Am I being reasonable? I was so excited to co-create a life with you and share the ups and downs together...but what you've done is...beyond crossing a boundary."

"Maybe we can try couple's counseling," he said hopefully.

She shook her head. "Are you serious? There's no counseling for this. You don't understand what protection is. It's one thing if you were an alcoholic or couldn't hold a job...but you put magic on me, Ron. Do you understand that?

Shanice continued, "Magic that you didn't understand or even think to ask questions about. You put me in danger and my son...my son will never recover from what you did. There's no version of this marriage that works out. I don't want to see you or hear your voice. Sometimes, I'm afraid I will physically harm you from my anger."

"Shanice, please."

"This is the right decision for me. And I know we can work together for Nakoa, but this is over. I'm going to take a walk now, give you some space—we both deserve someone who wants to figure it out together. And we're not that person for each other. We should probably tell Nakoa together..."

Blinking back tears, she walked out the door. Ron collapsed on the couch, overwhelmed with sadness. How had it come to this? How had he been pushed so far to have a child? Ron began to wail as Shanice left.

Nakoa was in an upbeat mood when he got home. His parents' grim expressions quickly brought his energy down.

"We need to talk, honey," Shanice said, bringing her son string cheese. "Let's go find your dad. I think he's in the living room. Ron!" she called.

Ron hadn't moved from the couch since his wife had left the house that morning. When he saw his son, he looked startled. Shanice gestured for him to begin. "Wake up, Ron, he's here."

"Nakoa," he said, "your mom and I have decided to divorce. We want to tell you that we plan on maintaining a friendship, and you will remain our son forever. I broke your mother's trust. I've tried...we've tried...to repair our relationship, but...we have found ourselves with emotions that are more difficult to resolve than expected. We are in a place that we never foresaw. And we think it's healthier for us to end it permanently."

"Is it my fault?" Nakoa said, eyes pricking with tears.

He knew that Marcus's presence had been hard on the family. But he hadn't realized that it would break up his parents' marriage. He felt horrible. This was all his fault.

"No, no, baby, of course not," Shanice said quickly. "Please don't think that. This happens sometimes. In life, relationships change. It doesn't mean your father and I don't love each other. But we can't be married anymore."

"Maybe you will take a break and get back together," Nakoa said, trying not to cry. "I heard that happens sometimes too."

Ron and Shanice shared a look.

"You know, son," Ron says. "I empathize. I really do."

"But I don't think that's going to happen," Shanice cut in quickly.

"You never know," Ron said. "Nakoa's right. Love works in mysterious ways. Sometimes people do rediscover how much they care for each other if they just take a little space."

He looked up at his wife hopefully, but she shook her head.

"That might be true," she said. "But it's not all that common. Certain things...cause people to break up permanently."

Ron's face fell. He looked crushed, and Nakoa felt his father's sadness radiate across the room. How could this be happening?

"On my birthday, too," he said.

"Son—" Ron said, but Nakoa was already pushing past him.

He ran upstairs to his room, carrying his heavy backpack over one shoulder. As soon as he got there, he flopped down on his bed and opened his physics textbook.

He was more determined than ever to study and become something great. He knew that all he had to do was make it to college, preferably a school far away from Georgia.

Marcus's face and his raspy, cackling voice still haunted him. He felt like his evil twin had ruined his life—and now, his parents' lives too.

That wasn't the only thing that troubled him, though. He hated to admit it, but he'd gotten used to having Marcus around. He'd become familiar. With his twin there, Nakoa was never alone. He wondered if Marcus were easier to bear than his sense of loneliness. He'd always had someone to talk to, even if that someone was rude and mean-spirited. Now, he was certain to be lonely. Part of him—a gross, shameful part—almost wished Marcus was there. He wondered what Marcus would say about his parents' divorce. He wondered how Marcus would feel. He wondered where Marcus had gone.

Was Marcus really part of him now? Before disappearing, he'd claimed that he'd always live inside of Nakoa. Was he there? Nakoa rubbed the center of his chest in a circular motion. Were some of the things he did or thought because of Marcus? Would he always carry that darkness with him?

He shoved the longing for Marcus as far down as he could. It was gross. Marcus was gross. He'd killed his dog. He'd ruined his friendships. He caused his parents' divorce. He wished none of that had ever happened.

He didn't miss his twin at all. Did he?

20th BIRTHDAY

It was Nakoa's first year of college, and he was thriving. After the wild events of his teenage years, he'd finally come into his own. Now he was pursuing a degree at Caltech in Pasadena, California. He wasn't sure yet what major he'd choose. He was leaning toward physics, but chemistry and engineering were also contenders. Whatever he chose, he was definitely going into the sciences. English wasn't his strongest subject, and he'd chosen Caltech for a reason.

Part of him wanted to try to find a scientific explanation for what had happened to him. His father's stories of hexes and witchcraft were entertaining but outlandish. He simply didn't believe them. Nakoa believed in science. He believed in reason. He knew there had to be logic behind Marcus's appearance. Even if he was a weird medical freak of nature, it would make him feel better to know that and be able to put a name to it.

Pasadena had been a good change for him. It was nothing like Atlanta, and it felt like a fresh start in every possible way. He was learning to surf now—

Nakoa, surfing!—and he'd started to adopt some of the easy-going California lifestyles of his peers—hip hop, taco trucks, surfing, and Dodgers games. He felt like a new person. Relaxed Nakoa. Nakoa who'd never had an evil twin pop out of his chest. No one at Caltech had heard about Marcus, and he didn't tell anyone.

In his free time, he'd joined the campus robotics team. They were developing a new type of drone, and the work was exciting. He didn't know much about robots yet, but he was learning fast. He considered putting his name forward for team leader next year.

He'd met a girl there. Danielle was a first-year like him and a brilliant engineer. She already knew what she wanted to do with her life. On their first date—a quick excursion to Pinkberry after a troubleshooting session on the drone—she'd told him she wanted to work for NASA someday. He'd never met anyone like her: smart, naturally beautiful, driven, and funny. Every time he saw Danielle, he felt as if she was glowing. Her face was perfectly lit at all times. Sometimes she didn't seem real. Their first kiss hadn't gone well. Nakoa accidentally bit her lip. Instead of making the bite a big deal, Danielle joked that Nakoa was hungry, which put him at ease and made him feel less embarrassed.

He'd also met a guy. Now that he was out of his parents' house, he felt more comfortable exploring his bisexuality, bisexuality that Marcus had confirmed to him years prior, which he tried to suppress. Jarrett was his polar opposite: an applied mathematics major who had more talent than sense. He was less organized and methodical than Danielle, but he was a whole lot of fun. They'd met at a bar in Pasadena with a group of freshmen during Nakoa's first week of school. It was his first time at a bar at all—much less talking to a man—and he'd been reluctant to go. Nakoa was impressed with Jarrett because he was so straightforward.

With Danielle and Jarrett, Nakoa was nervous and awkward, but sincere and eager to explore what dating was all about. Part of Nakoa, an irrational part, was painfully nervous that Marcus would appear out of nowhere—like he was still possessed. He feared kissing Danielle or Jarrett to have Marcus reach through his shirt and grab ahold of their face.

It was as if having too much fun, going out on dates, hooking up, and meeting people, wasn't allowed. It felt too risky with his secret twin. After all, Marcus had first emerged on his birthday. He often wondered which of his love interests would be the most understanding of Marcus. He was unsure who could handle it best.

His friends had dragged him out, though, and he was glad they had. Jarrett had instantly caught his eye. He danced wildly, better than anyone else on the dance floor. Jarrett was free-spirited and did what he wanted at all times. Jarrett had magnetizing qualities in spite of their differences. In some ways, they complemented each other well. Jarrett had initiated their first kiss, and it had been passionate.

Nakoa had never had a girlfriend or boyfriend besides his childhood crush Perstefania and didn't know how everything worked. Danielle and Jarrett were so different from each other and required a personalized approach. His parents' relationship was the only reference he had. They had never spoken to him about dating and never broached the topic of sex. Little did he know that his mother had been tracking his romantic interests and internet search history since his youth. Nakoa wasn't sure whether he preferred Jarrett or Danielle. He felt pressured to choose one of them as the dates progressed, and he learned more about their lives. He often felt a deep fear of missing out if he decided to become serious with either of them.

Danielle was the safe choice—the one who made more sense. He could build a stable life with her; he knew he would not be discriminated against publicly and was sure his parents would approve of the match. But Jarrett felt more exciting. He was a wild card. Nakoa knew he'd never be bored with him around. Still, he couldn't anticipate what his parents would think if he brought Jarrett home. He couldn't envision if they had even heard about bisexuality. He decided that he would base his decision, not on whom he liked more, but on whoever was most accepting of his deep secret—the secret that lurked in the shadows of his heart. He would determine this through social experiments.

Despite his hopes, his parents had never gotten back together. They'd gone through with the divorce, and as soon as the decision was made, things moved quickly. Ron moved out, and Nakoa had lived with his mom for the rest of his last year of high school. The house had been different without his father around. Lonelier. Sadder. Part of him didn't want to go back for Christmas—things were too different—but he knew skipping Christmas would break his parents' hearts.

His phone buzzed, and he looked down.

Speak of the devil.

It was Ron. He'd left a voicemail. Taking a deep breath, Nakoa pressed the phone to his ear and hit play to listen to his father's message.

"Hey, son! This is dad. I wanna hear all about college. I miss you so much. I just had lunch with your mom, and don't tell her I told you, but she met a guy, and they're getting married. I'm so happy for her. She deserves to be happy, and he sounds like a good enough guy. Son, I love you so much. Call me back!"

Nakoa's face crumpled, and he inhaled, grounding himself. Much as he didn't want to admit it, he'd still held out hope that his parents would get back together. Now those hopes were dashed. Forcing his face into a smile, he dialed his father back.

"Hey, Dad!"

"Son! You sound well. Making waves with the ladies of Caltech?"

Nakoa winced in awkwardness. He didn't feel ready to tell his father he was bi yet.

"Somethin' like that..." he responded. "Many ladies and many..."

"Did you get my voicemail?" Ron interjected.

He sighed. "Yep. So. Mom, huh?"

"She seems really happy."

"How did they even meet?"

He knew he sounded sort of hostile. But he didn't like the thought of his mom with someone else. He didn't want a new dad. He liked the one he had. Sure, Ron had made some mistakes—but so had everyone. Marcus wasn't his fault. Privately, Nakoa felt like his mom blamed his father too much for what had happened. It didn't feel fair since he felt his dad was trying to help. Without his help, he would not exist.

"They met in a tennis club or somethin'," Ron said. "He was facing off against her one day, and I guess she was impressed with his racket skills."

Nakoa made a disgusted face as his dad spoke. He was happy his dad couldn't see him.

"Tennis, Dad?" he said. "That's kinda lame!"

"I know it might not be what you're used to, but I think you'll really like him. You two could get along. It might not be so bad to have two dads, huh?"

"This new guy isn't my dad! He isn't even my stepdad. I'm too old for all of that." Nakoa said, more vehemently than he intended to.

There was a long silence at the other end of the line.

"Look, Nakoa," his father said gently. "The last few years have been difficult for you...for all of us. No one knows that more than me. But we're moving forward together. As a family. And when I say you'll like this guy, when I say your mother's really happy, please trust me. I know your mom very well—she's happy. We all just want the best for you—for everyone."

Nakoa sighed and took a deep breath. He knew his father was right. It had been hard seeing Ron move into a tiny apartment. It had been hard not seeing him as much as he wanted, but they had to move forward.

"You're right, Dad," he said. "I'm not being fair. I'll give him a chance. And we'll all move forward. As a family."

21ˢᵗ BIRTHDAY

Shanice and her new husband glowed, twirling around under string lights and jazz music as one hundred formal clad guests looked on and smiled. A large tent had been set up in the Peachtree home's backyard. Shanice had obtained the house in the divorce. Nakoa, who was approaching his 21st birthday, had visibly changed again. After playing basketball and working out regularly, Nakoa had lowered his blood pressure and lost nearly eighty pounds since Marcus left.

Nakoa was lean. He was proportionate and no longer at risk for heart failure or diabetes. Reconnecting with old friends and seeing a therapist resulted in calmness and confidence, apparent in Nakoa's smile and demeanor. He was now one year away from completing an Applied Physics program at Caltech in Pasadena, California, and was offered the largest book publishing deal in history. He had also grown a full beard.

"Isn't this beautiful?"

Ron and Nakoa sat at a table swarming with poinsettias. Heat lamps, fragrant lavender misters, and electric mosquito traps had been set up to ensure the guests' comfort. Shanice and her new husband danced as guests socialized and took photos. Ron observed several wedding guests staring at Nakoa, pointing, and making comments.

An older man passed by their table, patting Nakoa on the back before saying, "I never believed the hype. Can't believe they'd hide such a handsome fella..." Nakoa kindly smiled at the man.

Ron looked over to his son and said, "I'm so happy for your mom...after what she's been through with me. I wanted you so bad that I was willing to do anything. Anything! I never thought about how my actions would affect her as the person carrying you."

"You were trying to help, Dad. Three miscarriages and a stillbirth would drive anyone to the extremes."

Ron continued, "Thank you for saying that. It was a lot, and we were almost five years older than you are now. So young. Son, relationships are not about one person—remember that. I should have asked her if what I was doing would actually make her happy. I didn't want to risk the IVF treatment not working. Relationships are ebb and flow. Yin and Yang." Ron took a sip of ginger beer. "So does my son have a special lady? I should say, 'Does my handsome, rich, educated son...'"

"Dad." Nakoa paused. "I'm bisexual."

"Nakoa Jamar...ya know..." Ron contemplated for a second. "...from the moment you were born, the exact moment your little legs came out, and we saw your huge eyes, we knew you were a warrior—a miracle. When I met you, all I could do was thank God. I just fell to my knees, thanking God for allowing me to have a child against these odds."

Ron's eyes began to tear. "So, thank you for telling me. I thank God for putting you in my life no matter who or what you are, you were or become. Back then, yesterday, today, and tomorrow."

Nakoa continued, "You're not mad or weirded out?"

"You're not mad or weirded out by me and all we've been through?"

Ron grabbed his son, hugging him tightly. "Son, I love that you see the warrior in yourself."

Ron and Nakoa watched his mom twirl like a princess. Ron continued, "Is this a new development?"

Nakoa took a breath. "Not really. After grandma's death, the divorce, the new marriage." Nakoa paused. "Marcus..." Nakoa touched his chest before continuing, "I learned many lessons. Do you think I should tell mom?"

"Yes, tell your mom."

Ron high-fived his son. Ron and Nakoa continued to watch the dance before Shanice quickly ran off the dance floor to the bathroom. The band stopped playing music.

"Uh oh," Ron said, looking on.

An elderly woman passed Shanice vomiting in the bathroom. "Looks like a double congratulations are in order."

Shanice looked at the woman menacingly. "I'm sorry, honey, I've had five of them."

Shanice returned to the dance floor, gazing through the bright stage lights and analyzing the crowd to locate Ron. She began to scratch her chest.

"Hold on, son." Ron excused himself to a quiet space. He began to scroll through photos on his phone. Scrolling and scrolling, Ron finally located images of the napkins Ambrosia had written. He re-read the conditions of the egg spell over and over, scratching his head. Ron dialed Ambrosia, who picked up and immediately hung up. He dialed again. Ambrosia picked up and hung up.

Ron texted:

Hey, you! I know it's been years, but the egg thing. There's no issue with the whole light and dark thing?

What? Ambrosia responded.

We divorced a few years back, so she can't get pregnant, right? We gave the boys the egg and water from the pond to end the spell, Ron texted.

I wrote it down. Ron, you can't pay attention to details for the life of you = selfish.

Ron sent Ambrosia a photo of the napkin. She did not respond. Ron texted the picture of the napkin again. No response. He called Ambrosia, who picked up and immediately hung up.

The ellipsis appeared like she was texting. Several seconds went by, the ellipsis appearing and disappearing with no message.

Ambrosia finally sent a message, *What is happening?*

She's scratching her chest.

Then she must be pregnant. She's fertile until she dies. Not just from your little swimmers. I wrote it down. Lose my number.

Ron sent multiple texts to Ambrosia before noticing he had been blocked. Ron re-read the napkin photo which said:

Marcus will go back inside of Nakoa. Feed this egg to both boys. Give them water from the mirror pond to drink. Conditions:

- Shanice will be fertile until she dies. If she has another child, darkness will become visible when the child enters puberty and/or Shanice herself. This is the agreement.

He rushed back to the table. Several people were speaking to Nakoa about news stories they had heard about him over the years.

"Hey, bud, where's Mom?" Ron asked Nakoa.

"I'm right here."

"Mommmmm!" Nakoa shouted.

"What?" Shanice"s chin slowly moved down as she stared at Nakoa.

A tiny face began to emerge between Shanice's cleavage through blood and puss. Its head moved in maniacal circles, forming a neck, its menacing eyes staring at Nakoa and Ron. The onlooking guests screamed as limbs quickly formed and began to crawl out of Shanice's chest.

The End

The End

Ross Victory is a singer/songwriter turned author from Southern California. He is the author of the award-winning non-fiction books *Views from the Cockpit: The Journey of a Son* and *Panorama: The Missing Chapter.* When Ross isn't writing or singing, he enjoys traveling and cars.

Learn more: rossvictory.com

Also Available